FROM THE AUTHOR OF THE LEGENDS
OF LEEPER HOLLER SERIES..

URBAN

LEGENDS

OF

LINCOLN

COUNTY

MISSOURI

VOLUME 2.0

NORMAN MCFADDEN

Norman McFadden

I0562127

URBAN
LEGENDS
OF
LINCOLN
COUNTY
MISSOURI

VOLUME 2.0

POLSTON HOUSE

NORMAN MCFADDEN

Norman McFadden

URBAN LEGENDS OF LINCOLN COUNTY
MISSOURI VOLUME 2
Copyright © 2022 by Norman McFadden. All rights
reserved.

Published by Polston House Publishing, LLC.
www.Polstonhouse.com

Book design copyright © 2022 by Polston House Publishing,
LLC. All rights reserved.

Published in the United States of America

Contents

1

George Washington Cottle

It was February 28, 1836, and the cold wind was blowing from the north, bringing the temperature down to 36 degrees. The brave volunteers fighting at the Alamo were so cold that their fingers could Hardly pull the triggers, or reload the guns. This was the beginning of the Texas war for independence from Mexico which lasted 13 days at the Alamo.

The battle was located near present day San Antonio, Texas. Over 1000 Mexican forces came against the Alamo that day led by General Antonio Lopez De Santa Anna, with only 200 volunteers defending the Alamo. Commanded by Jim Bowie and William Travis, farmer Frontiersman Davy Crockett, and James Bonham.

The battle raged on for 13 grueling days. Jim Bowie, William Travis, James Bonham, and David Crockett all died in this courageous battle along with 200 Rangers. After the battle, General Antonio ordered his soldiers to go out in the nearby Forest to gather wood. They carried it to Alamede Road. The next day at 3 p.m., they carried the bodies of the brave defenders of the Alamo to a big pile of wood. They stacked wood on the bodies and then burnt them that evening at 8 p.m.

You're asking yourself, "What does the Alamo have to do with Lincoln County?" Along with all of the brave men that died at the Alamo, there was a man that was born in Lincoln County, Missouri. He died on March 6, 1836. He was only 25 years old. On March 31, 1836, his twin Sons were born 25 days after he fell in the battle. Their names were Thomas Jackson Cottle and George Washington Cottle Jr.

This man that I'm talking about was a man that was born in 1811 here in the Hurricane township of Lincoln County, Missouri. This man was named George Washington Cottle and his father was Jonathan Cottle, and his mother was Margaret Cottle. We should be proud of our pioneers that settled in this part of the country. All of those who made the country what it is today, so that we can live in freedom and independence. I salute you George Washington Cottle, you gave your life so we could live in Freedom. The good people of Lincoln County know this; freedom is not free.

Joshua 1:9

"Have I not commanded you? Be strong and courageous, do not be afraid, do not be discouraged, for the Lord your God will be with you wherever you go."

2

The Legend of the Lost Cabin

One day as I sat at home watching the wildlife out in my backyard, the phone rang. When I answered a voice said, "Hello, have you ever heard the story about the lost cabin in the woods?" The voice sounded like that of a kindly older gentleman. I told him that I hadn't and asked him to go ahead and tell me. This is the story he told.

In the year 1905 a man and a woman, named John and Suzanne, from Hawk Point, Missouri, got married. Sadly, they were both very anti-social and liked to live like hermits. Shortly after they were wedded they bought some property far out in the woods with the hopes that no one would ever find them, and that they could live in complete isolation. John built them a cabin from the trees that he cut down on their land. The tale says that they had a little baby girl and named her Josie. Though no one could be certain because they almost never came into town.

Josie was said to be the most perfect baby, and as she grew, she became quite beautiful. She had long silken blonde hair and sparkling sky blue eyes. But she knew nothing of people other than her parents, having never left their property. When Josie was around 12 years old she ran into a lady in the backwoods named Jessica. This Jessica, was known as the local witch. She had all kinds of herbs and spices for magic potions and spells. And she practiced witchcraft out in those woods.

Now I don't know if you folks know it or not, but there are white witches and then there are dark witches. A white witch practices white magic and believes that they are helping people, and a dark witch uses demons to do her bidding, creating evil spells and doing harm to others.

Jessica was a dark witch. She would travel the woods far and wide searching for the right ingredients for her magical brews. And this was how she came across Josie one day. For almost two years the two would meet secretly while Jessica taught Josie her terrible trade.

Josie was around 14 when it happened, she had been helping Jessica with a spell when something went wrong. They knew it the moment it happened, something came straight up out of the pits of hell and went right into Josie. The demon knocked her to the ground as it entered her body. Jessica watched as this beautiful fourteen year old girl's face twisted and changed and a large hump came up on her back. Jessica couldn't watch any longer and ran from the scene, leaving the child laying on the ground.

It was the next day before Josie's parents found her frail body lay on the ground where the demon had knocked her. Josie woke and began behaving as if she had lost her mind. Her parents couldn't understand how this thing was their sweet, lovely daughter. John and Suzanne had to fight and drag her back home, all the while she screamed and bit and kicked at them.

When they finally got her home they chained her to the bed in her room, not knowing what else to do. Then they barred her window. They felt that this was the only way to keep her from hurting herself or escaping. Their mistake was that they didn't seek help and they tried to figure out what to do on their own.

Not quite a month later, the situation came to a boiling point. As evening came so did a terrible thunderstorm, the lightning flashed and the wind howled, the thunder shook the tiny cabin. John and Suzanne did not hear Josie break free of her chains. Suddenly she was in the doorway to the living room. One can only imagine what she did to her parents, as I am not going to write such a horror here. After she had finished with her parents she ran off into the woods.

It was Jessica who found John and Suzanne some time later, she didn't want anyone to know about what had happened, so she quietly buried the bodies, and no one knew any different because of how reclusive they were. Ten years later as Jessica lay on her deathbed she hearkened unto the Lord Jesus and asked forgiveness. But the guilt of this tragedy had to be told, so she recanted the story to her own relatives as they sat around her deathbed. She told them that even to that day Josie was still possessed by the demons and called the log cabin her home.

The man on the phone seemed distant as he finished the story and gave me directions to the lost cabin. The next day I headed out to see if there was any sign of truth out in those woods. I headed to the Southwest corner of Lincoln County out along Big Creek. I hiked for almost a full two days searching for that cabin with no luck. But then at the end of the second day as the sun was giving up the last of its light I found the cabin. I think I was only able to find it because I, at this point, was lost. As the last of the daylight quickly faded I had a terrible realization. There would be no way for me to find my way back to my car in the dark. I only had one option, to stay in the cabin overnight.

Now I have done some dumb things in my life, but I think that decision might have been the dumbest. I would have been better off out in the woods, even without a tent. I quickly looked around inside and immediately began blessing the house, pouring a little anointing oil at each window and door.

Things were quiet until the midnight hour when all Hell broke loose. First there was scratching sounds along the doors, next whatever it was that wanted in began to scream like a banshee. But there was nothing I could do, whatever was outside that cabin was mad. And I have to admit that this reporter was about scared to death! I began to pray, because I certainly wasn't going to be sleeping. Around 3 a.m. I couldn't take it any longer, so I quickly grabbed my things and decided that I was going to make a run for it. I just knew that I had to get away from that cabin.

I made it to the front door and stopped cold in my tracks. The realization hit me, whatever was outside could not come in. It could not pass the windows and doors that had been blessed with oil and prayed over. If I wanted to make it out alive, I would have to stay inside for the rest of the night. Suddenly it was as if the Devil himself had unleashed the most horrifying depths of hell right outside that little cabin in those isolated woods. But I knew that it was the prayer of the Blood of Jesus that kept them outside those thin, nearly dilapidated walls. I thought I might lose my mind that night as I sat on the floor and prayed and prayed.

Things seemed to quiet down when suddenly the front door flew open, I ran and shut it. By the time I turned around the window popped up in its frame. As I ran over to shut it, I looked out in to the black night. It was too dark, I could see nothing.

Then something happened that froze me in place. I couldn't move a muscle. In the dark woods that surrounded the cabin, came a quiet, soft whisper, calling my name over and over again. "Norman, Norman let me in." I slammed the window shut and went back to where I had been sitting. I covered my ears and began to pray out loud, Lord Jesus wrap your arms around me and protect me!

Over and over I prayed the same thing until finally the first rays of dawn's light broke over the horizon, breaking the hold the darkness had on the land. The demons fled with the darkness as they despise the light and prefer to lurk in the darkness of the night.

In a matter of moments I was out of the cabin and back into the sunlit woods, heading right toward the rising sun. I knew that I had entered the woods from the east, so I got my bearings and bolted. I moved as fast as I could through the woods only resting when I had to. Almost three hours later I found Big Creek, then followed it for another thirty minutes right to my car. I drove off quickly without looking back, and I don't plan on ever going out there again!

Mark 5:2-5

"And when He had come out of the boat, immediately there met Him out of the tombs a man with an unclean spirit, who had his dwelling among the tombs; and no one could bind him, not even with chains, because he had often been bound with shackles and chains. And the chains had been pulled apart by him, and the shackles broken in pieces; neither could anyone tame him. And always, night and day, he was in the mountains and in the tombs, crying out and cutting himself with stones."

Evil spirits are real, and they will inhabit your body if you let them. But if you are covered by the blood of Jesus then they cannot touch you.

Norman McFadden

3

Old Liberty Cemetery

From the Cradle to the Grave. It's a journey that we must all take. And we all have choices on how we live our lives along the way. Two things that none of us have a choice about though, is to be born and to die.

I was visiting a friend of mine named Jim Mudd out in Millwood, Missouri. He told me a story about a graveyard that was on Old School Road. He told me that something "Supernatural" was going on out there in that graveyard. He said that he and a few of his friends were out there coon hunting one night. In a nervous kind of voice he continued;

"We went by the old Liberty Cemetery around 1 a.m. There was some stuff going on in that little spooky graveyard. We just could not explain what was happening." He did not go into details about what it was that he had seen. I could tell that he was quite nervous about the situation though. I did not pressure him for more

17

information. I figured that if he wanted me to know more, he would have told me.

So I told Jim that I would go out there and do some investigative research. We said our goodbyes and I left his place to plan my trip out to the Old Liberty Cemetery. It wasn't until about a month later that I was available to go. My grandson decided to go along with me and keep me company. We arrived at the cemetery on a cold and windy November evening around 6pm.

The moon was bright and full, so we could see clearly. Our plan was to stay the night in the car. I told my grandson that I was going to take a little walk around the cemetery to see if I could spot anything out of the ordinary. It was so eerily quiet that night out among the graves, except for the wind whistling through the treetops. You could certainly feel the chill of winter moving in.

It was so quiet at times you could have heard a pin drop. As I opened the large metal gate it let out an irritating squeak that was so loud it hurt my ears. As the clouds fled away, the moonlight illuminated the tombstones in that little graveyard. They appeared to be glowing in the light of the full moon.

I walked around the little cemetery with my little flashlight in hand. I could read the names on the tombstones, as well as the dates. Some of them were so old that the writing had vanished from the face of the tombstone. From the dates that I could read, it looked like 75% of the people buried there were young. Many under the age of 17.

We have all heard that "God sends angels to watch over children while they're sleeping." There were many families buried there, here are a few of the names. Abbott,

Anson, Besterfeldt, Brandenburg, Carter, Green, Henderson, Lewallen, Mabry, Porter, and last but not least Williams. Names of pioneer families that made it possible for us to be able to call Lincoln County home.

I imagined the sacrifices they had to make to settle in an untamed country. I went back to my car with a sense of pride swelling up within me. We sat in the car for a while and kept a close eye on the graveyard. We had not seen a single movement, so we started telling scary ghost stories to each other.

I guess it was around 12:30 a.m., when we saw something that looked like a small cloud rising up like a lost spirit from one of the graves. And then another cloud, and another. They just kept coming up from the graves. It Looked like about 15 or 20 wisps of small clouds floating over the cemetery. They hovered over the graves like a mother hawk soaring in the sky watching over her young.

They were floating about 10 feet or 15 feet above the tombstones. I scrambled to find my cell phone. Once I found it, I took pictures of the floating clouds. For some strange reason or another, none of the pictures showed anything. They were just black pictures, nothing at all in the photos. The clouds continued floating over the graves as we sat there watching.

My grandson looked so scared, he was as white as a ghost. But for me, my curiosity was going wild, like a fire in California that was out of control. I just had to get a closer look and see what this was all about. So I got out of the car, and walked toward the cemetery. As I opened the gate, it let out that irritating squeak again. The whistling wind seemed to carry it's echo off into the night. Surely to give a chill to the bones of any poor soul that might hear it.

Suddenly, something happened. I don't scare easy, but I had become very nervous. As I walked through the darkness, I said to myself' "I will fear no evil because my God will protect me." I started walking slower, and slowly creeping closer, and closer to the clouds. They looked like they were gathering in one big group on the north side of the cemetery.

This may sound a little crazy, but I was thinking that they were watching me. I could feel this eerie sick feeling coming up from the bottom of my stomach. I felt the hair stand up on the back of my neck, and I had a chill running up and down my spine. I heard the wind start to pick up. The whistling of it was blowing through the trees now, and it sounded just like a train whistle.

The large mass of clouds started floating towards me. I immediately decided that I didn't need to get a closer look after all. I turned and headed back to my car as fast as I possibly could. I made it through that old cemetery gate so quick that I don't recall hearing it squeak. I opened the door of my car and started the engine. I threw the vehicle in gear then I got the heck out of there!

I cannot explain what I saw there that night. I suppose that one might say that it could have been fog. Just a mass of low hanging clouds with the wind blowing them around in circles above the graves. There could also be some sort of spring running under the cemetery causing a formation of clouds above it after the ground cools at night.

Whatever the case may be, I agree with Jim. It certainly seemed like something supernatural was going on in that little Cemetery. Perhaps it was evidence of guardian angels watching over children as they are sleeping.

Matthew 18:10
"See that you do not despise these little one, for I tell you that in heaven Their angels always behold the face of my father who is in heaven."

Norman McFadden

4

Philemon Plummer

This story is about a family feud that resulted in the death of two of the family members. It was a family feud that didn't amount to a hill of beans, but it got way out of hand. The year was 1839, and it was springtime. It was a warm April day and the wind was blowing quietly across the hillside.

The Plummer family lived on some land on a cliff located about a mile West of Kingdom Lake in Lincoln County, not far from the Mississippi River. Philemon Plummer had let his children (they had six) go and play at his father's house just up the road. When they got back home that one warm evening, they reported to their dad, Philemon, that a slave lady that belonged to his father had insulted them.

Then his sister Anna took the slave lady's side against the children. Philemon was upset, so he grabbed two of his children for witnesses and headed to his father's house. When he got there, they were all setting on the porch enjoying the evening breeze. He confronted his dad about the problem and ordered his dad to whip the slave lady.

When his dad refused to whip her, Philemon proceeded to do it himself. The slave lady was standing in the yard, so he started to go out and begin whipping her. His sister Anna Baker stepped in between him and the lady. Philemon tried to move his sister aside so he could get to the lady.

His sister retaliated by hitting him three to four times in the mouth during the altercation. He grabbed both of his sister's hands so she wouldn't be able to hit him anymore. Joseph, his brother, seen him grabbing Anna's hands so he ran out to help her. Joseph grabbed a rock from out of the yard and threatened to hit Philemon in the head if he didn't let Anna go.

With a lot of cussing and screaming in the yard, Philemon shoved Anna to the ground. Anna hit the ground and she took a look around for something to use in her defense. She saw an old Pioneer pitchfork. For those who do not know what a Pioneer pitchfork is, it has a handle about seven foot long which comes to a metal fork that has three prongs about an inch in diameter.

She picked up the pitchfork and charged toward Philemon. He managed to get the Pitchfork away from Anna and shoved her down again. Then out of the corner of his eye, he noticed Joseph had raised a rock back and he thought he was going to get hit with it. Having the pitchfork in his hand, he swung it around and hit Joseph upside the head. Joseph fell to the ground and died from the injury.

Philemon was arrested by the Sheriff and booked on the murder of his brother. If that's not enough grief for the Plummer family, Joseph Sr., their father, scraped enough money together to come up with Philemon's bail. So he gave it to his other son John to go to town and get Philemon out of jail.

On the way to town the son was robbed of the money and killed. In less than a week the Plummer family had two sons that were murdered and another one in jail. Philemon was indicted for the murder of his brother and he was found guilty of manslaughter in the third degree. He served three years in the Missouri State Penitentiary. Upon his release Philemon moved his family across the Mississippi River to Calhoun County. He remained there until his death in 1855 at the age of 53. He is buried in Calhoun County at Plummer's graveyard on a hill close to the Mississippi. His family stayed in Lincoln County, Missouri. This story should remind you to think about what you're doing before you do it. Don't let your anger overcome your common sense.

This story was taken from a book published in 1888 called "The History of Lincoln County, Missouri."

Ephesians 6:1-4

"Children, obey your parents in the Lord, for this is right. Honor your father and your mother which is the first commandment with a promise- that it may go well with you and that you may enjoy long life on the Earth. Fathers, do not exasperate your children, instead bring them up in the training and instructions of the Lord."

Norman McFadden

5

Private David Clark

Most people have never heard of Private David Clark, but after this article you will know who he is. Private David Clark was the son of Christopher Columbus Clark, the first pioneer in the area of Moscow Mills in Lincoln County, Missouri. Although Private David Clark did not die in Lincoln County, he did die fighting to protect our way of life. From Moscow Mills, Missouri this hero went to Texas to become a Ranger. His story was long in the making and should have been written a long time before now.

The story begins in late 1836. The Republic of Texas issued an order to create three Ranger companies to protect the inhabitants living on the frontier from marauding natives. Company B of the Texas Rangers was under the command of Captain Thomas H. Berron, and was stationed out of Fort Milam near the present day Falls County.

A scout searching for sign of natives in the area reported that there were trails about twelve miles from the Fort. Sergeant George B. Erath started out to locate the native camp with only ten rangers and three citizen volunteers. As they came up a ridgeline, they could see the native camp spread out below them.

January 7th dawned cold for Texas as the sun slowly broke the darkness as it rose over the hill. The Rangers tied their horses and proceeded on foot to within rifle range of the camp. The Sergeant counted around a hundred native men and their dogs making their way up toward the Rangers. Knowing that they were outnumbered at least nine to one, Sergeant Erath ordered the attack. He hoped that since they had the high ground that they had the advantage, but it proved to be a bad call on his part.

On that cold January day, as the first shots rang out the natives were caught by surprise. Initial shots killed and wounded several of the natives, but they quickly rallied when they discovered that they had the upper hand by their number of men. The native warriors charged full speed toward the Texas Rangers.

Private David Clark, was one of the volunteers and he was wounded. During the battle Sergeant Erath and Private McLochian found the wounded David Clark. Private McLochian's rifle had become broken during the battle, not thinking of himself Private David Clark offered his rifle to the other Private. Now that's just like someone from Moscow Mills, Missouri, to put others before themselves. McLochian refused and ran up the hill to the other Rangers. Sergeant Erath stayed with the wounded man a little longer, but lost his courage when he saw another dozen native warriors coming their way. The Sergeant ran up the hill leaving Clark wounded and defenseless.

Rumor has it that Clark took his rifle and lasted as long as his bullets did. When the Rangers later returned they found Clark scalped and his hands cut off. In my eyes Private David Clark died as a true Missourian, fighting until the last bullet and his last breath.

David Clark had enlisted in Coloniel Burleson's Mounted Rangers and had served under Captain Hill from July 3rd, 1836 until September 11th, 1836 when he was transferred to Captain Berron's Company B. Private David Clark was reportedly from Moscow Mills in Lincoln County, Missouri. He was born March 22nd 1796 and died January 7th 1837. Private David Clark was survived by his wife and son.

Private Clark I salute you, a true hero.

2 Timothy 4:7
"I have fought the good fight, I have finished the race, I have kept the faith."

Norman McFadden

6

The Cuivre River on Fire

Have you ever heard of the song "Smoke on the Water?" This story is about an incident involving smoke on the water at the Cuivre River just west of Old Monroe, Missouri. You might ask yourself, "How can the river burn if it is made up of water?" Not only was it on fire, but it burnt two men to death.

It happened on a hot summer day in 1954. The warm wind was blowing from the south. The birds were singing their songs and the flowers were blooming and releasing a beautiful smell into the air. It was a season that brings lovers together, but something deadly was leaking into the Cuivre river.

The Phillips 66 oil pipe line had sprung a leak and no one knew until it was too late. It wasn't until someone saw the black smoke rolling from a distance. They knew that the fire was real close to the Cuivre River. They thought that it might be a risk for anyone or anything along the bank of the river. So they drove out there and saw that the river was on fire.

At the time, the river was overflowing the banks. Because there had been a lot of rain and the river was up. The Saint Charles Fire Department was the first ones on the scene. They knew you couldn't use water to put fire out on water. So they started fighting it by squirting wood foam onto it. They knew they had to control it before it got to the bridge.

Before long there were five Fire Departments on the scene fighting this out of control fire on the river. Black rolling smoke filled the sky and it could be seen all the way from Troy. Frank Lauritzen, and Jess Kelly brought their boats over to help extinguish the fire before it reached the bridge.

Frank's boat got a little too close to the fire. The water swept over the boat filling it full of fire and water. As the boat capsized, the men were scared of drowning or burning. The smoke was so heavy they could hardly see anything. Others heard Frank hollering so they found him and dragged him out to the bank. They kept searching for the other two, they found one who was still alive and they drove them to the bank. As he laid there he told the man how cold it was. But it was really a hot day. And then he said he felt like he was under water, right before he slipped away.

The other man was not found until the next day after the fire was put out. It was said that he was burned so bad he was unrecognizable. The good news was that they kept it from reaching the bridge over Highway 79. This is a story that has been passed down from generation to generation. It is based on the true account, but with every story, comes a possibility of variation.

Isaiah 43:2
"When you passed through the water, I'll be with you; when you pass through the Rivers they will not sweep over you. And when you walk through the fire you will not burn. The blade will not set you a fire."

7

The Curse on Lincoln County

I wrote a story a few years ago about the screaming chimney. The story of Simeon Thornhill, dead by the hands of his slave Giles. Before you read the story, I know that slavery was wrong, and that you do not judge anyone by the color of their skin. There is only one race in my eyes and that's the human race.

Sometimes we have to look back to go forward. To make sure that we don't make the same mistakes again. Thornhill and Giles were drinking and got into an argument over a disagreement. Giles came to kill Simeon Thornhill in Thornhill's qwn yard. He stabbed him with a kitchen knife several times. And that is when the curse began.

To enjoy this story you need to read the Legend of the Screaming Chimney in the first urban legends of Lincoln County Missouri book. They took Giles and put him in jail in Troy Missouri. That is when the curse begins when friends and kinfolk took matters into their own hand. It was on the second day after Thornhill's death, it being January 1, 1859, the mob assembled and went into Troy.

In the afternoon, James Callaway stepped out onto the front porch of the "Horse Block" near where Mr. Heart's store was and made a short speech to the crowd that was there. The crowd started whooping and hollering and screaming "We want justice for Thornhill!"

And then they made their way up to the jailhouse on Main Street.. When they got to the jail house Captain Salle was waiting with a shotgun because he already heard about the crowd. They quickly overtook him and yanked away the gun. They demanded the key to the cell, but Captain Salle refused.

So as few of the men stayed there to keep an eye on Captain Salle, others went downtown to get some tools to break into the jail. When they returned with the tools they proceeded to make their way into the jail. James Callaway, James Segrass, and Samuel Carter made their way into the jail house and dragged Giles out into the jailhouse yard.

They had nailed a cross together and laid him up on it. They put his feet together and nailed a spike through them. They stretched his arms out upon the cross and tied them. A couple men had dug a hole in the yard and they picked up the cross and shoved It down in the hole, and filled in dirt around it.

They already had a little fire built out in the jailhouse yard. They started putting wood around the cross. James Segrass grabbed the hot poker from the fire they had built, and poked Giles's eyes out with the hot poker. They had never heard someone scream so loud in pain. And all the men just laughed about it. They lit the logs that were stacked around the cross. As he started screaming and the fire was burning him you could smell the burning flesh. The men stood there drinking and watching as he burned to death.

For some reason or another after the fire went out, one of the men hollered that they should reduce him to ash. So they lit the fire again even though he was dead they burnt him again.

No man has the right to take the law into his own hands. No man has the right to take another man's life. Revenge is mine says the Lord! It was March 25, 1859, they took the three leaders of the mob to the court of Lincoln County in Troy Missouri. The men named were James Callaway, James Gegrass, and Simeon Thornhill. They went to a jury trial and they found all three men not guilty. Then a week later they took others who were part of the mob. Their names were William Birch, James Reeds, Smith McGinnis, D. H. Cliambea, George Washington Stonebraker, John W. Rice, Gabriel Thompson, Charles Kimler, William Hoppens, Zach Lovelace, Glan G. Wilson, and James Horton.

But a jury of their peers found them not guilty. You would think that's the end of the story but it's not, God says revenge is mine. So after the court found all the men not guilty, there was a curse that came. Have you ever heard of generational curses? All the leaders of the mob died at a young age. The man who poked Giles eyes out, several of his children were born blind. The men involved in the mob all died from a violent death, except one that moved out of county.

This is just one of the men that was involved in the mob "George Washington Stonebreaker" died from a shot in the back of the head. What goes around will come around. You live by the sword you'll die by the sword. What you sow you will reap, and two wrongs don't make a right. This is the urban legend of the curse of Lincoln County Missouri.

Numbers 14:18

"The Lord is slow to anger, and abounding in steadfast love, forgiveness, iniquity and transgression, but he will by no means clear the guilty, visiting to inquiry of the father on the children to the 3rd or 4th generation."

8

The Ghost of Indian Camp Creek

Several people have called me and told me about a lurking teenage boy out at Indian Camp Creek. They said he never gets close enough to talk to and that he hides behind trees and bushes. He Just watches the kids from a distance as they play on the playground, and swimmers as they swim in Indian Camp Creek.

Some folks say that they have seen him walking up on the hills above the creek. People that picnic at the park said they'd seen him in other areas. One lady said she called out to him to see if he wanted some food and he just ran off. He stands at a distance from those who see him. Never speaking a word, he just watches them.

Miss Lewis, a camper with the Girl Scouts said he was dressed like a young man from the 1800's. A good-looking young man around 14 or 15 years old perhaps. This was just enough information to get this reporter's curiosity fired up. So I headed down to the Indian Camp Creek Park one morning to take a look around for myself.

If you have never been there, you go southeast on Highway 61 from Troy until you go across Big Creek and make the first right on Dietrich Road. There it's about a half a mile up on your right. It is a beautiful Park! I searched the creek first. I walked from one bridge to the other bridge by Hwy 61. I also searched the woods around the creek.

The first day I made it up to Cannon Cemetery. From daylight to dusk I searched until the park ranger told me I had to leave. The next day I came back and started again at the cemetery. While observing the names carved into the stones, I found a little boy that died there in this area before it was a park. The boy was 13 when he died. I searched and searched the name on my phone, and couldn't find the reason he died so young.

The Cannon family came to that area in 1811 and bought a hundred and eighty acres. They lived there as one big happy family. The little boy's name was Daniel Webster Cannon, and he was born on July 22, 1875. He died on March 20, 1888. His cause of death is unknown.

He had just become a teenager at the tender age of 13. His dad was George M. Cannon, and his mom's name was Sarah. The whole family is buried there at the park, in the cemetery. But I guess Daniel's spirit did not rest in peace. For some reason his spirit is still lurking around Indian Camp Creek Park.

This day I started searching up the other creek and the woods around it. I made it all the way up to the top of the hill on the right side of the park. But it was getting dark so I had to leave again. On the third day I searched the other side of the road on the left side from dusk to dawn. I found nothing. No ghost, and no teenage boy either.

There were a few times my mind played tricks on me and I thought I seen something behind the trees in the bushes and up on the hillside. Or was it the ghost that everyone had been seeing out there?

Altogether I spent four days searching and turned up empty handed, other than the information I discovered about the young boy who had died. But it was a good time in a beautiful park. If you get a chance to go down to Indian Camp Creek Park keep your eye out for the young boy. He might be in the woods, maybe behind the bushes or maybe just lurking up on the hill looking down at you. According to the people that go there his spirit still wanders the woods, the creek, and the playground.

2 Corinthians 5:8
"Absent from the body and present with the Lord."

That means when we die we go wherever we're going to go to spend eternity. Now every person has Spirits within them besides their own. And when they die, these Spirits go out looking for other hosts. These Spirits can take on the image of the person but it is not the person. Whoever dies goes on to meet their maker.

Norman McFadden

9

The Haunted Woods

This is like a story you have never heard before. It's about a young man that was very confused. This is the kind of story that as you are reading, you must make up your mind whether or not this young man was murdered or committed suicide.

Alright, here we go, fasten your seat belt and get ready for a story you will not forget. It was 1873 and on a Friday morning, Young Russell Henry had been working on the John Scott Farm. Russell got into a misunderstanding with John and told him he was going to kill him. John said he was going to go to Troy and have a warrant made out for Russell's arrest. So he headed out the front door. Russell Henry grabbed his shotgun and headed out the back door.

On his way out, he told his sister "here's my billfold and watch, hold it for me." It was a very odd request, but maybe young Henry thought he might lose his billfold and mess up his watch hunting. It was not very long and his sister heard four shots coming from the woods in the direction that Russell had gone. She ran to the front door to see if John had left yet.

It had been close to 15 minutes and he still hadn't gone to town to get that warrant. When she called him he came from the side of the house. She said "Would you please go check on Russell I think he might have done something stupid."

"He's alright," John said. "He's probably just out there shooting at squirrels." But he said not a word about going to town and getting the warrant now. The day went on and Russell did not come home for lunch. With a little encouragement from Russell's sister, John finally went looking for him.

He found him about a hundred and fifty yards behind the house. His body was leaning against a tree with what appeared to be two shotgun wounds to his head. Dr. Smith from Troy, came out and said it was a suicide. I guess back in them days they didn't know as much about suicide as they do these days. Because it's hard for someone to shoot their self twice in the head. Especially with a shotgun!

I went and looked for a criminal justice report. They say two shots to the head is only possible if you're assisted by someone else helping you. Suicide by multiple gunshots with a pistol have happened, but they are rare.

Now young Russell's family was very religious and suicide was an unforgivable sin. I could not find his grave or even the cemetery where he was buried. Russell Henry's spirit is still haunting them woods, I think. If it wasn't suicide, it was surely murder. There was only one person that had a reason and an opportunity to shoot him. Now you make up your mind. See if you think Russell Henry committed suicide or was murdered.

Think about the evidence I have presented and make up your own mind. Consider that double shot suicide is very, very rare. Unheard of with a shotgun. I'm not saying one way or the other though, it's up to you. The murder, or suicide, was committed right off of J Highway on Zoar Church Road. Just about halfway between Troy and Wright City, Missouri, back in the woods by a spring. So if you get back in them woods out there, watch out for Russell Henry's spirit. Until his murder is solved, he will wander the woods out there. You have been warned!

Matthew 12: 43
"When an evil spirit comes out of a man, it goes through dry places, seeking rest and does not find it."

Norman McFadden

10

The Legend of Alick Bailey

As we move forward, it is important to look back upon our history, including African American history. The African Americans have done so much for this country. They have helped to make this the greatest nation in the world. This is just one story of so many thousands which helped to grow and shape our nation. This story highlights an African American who grew up right here in Lincoln County, Missouri as a slave.

The year was 1848 and on a plantation in Cap Au Gris, Missouri was born a little baby boy. This little baby boy had no idea what his destination in life was going to be. His mother named him Alick Bailey, his last name taken from his owner, who was also the first sheriff of Lincoln County, Missouri, Mr. David Bailey. This little baby had no idea, but one day he was going to touch the hearts of many, and make the lives of the black community just a little bit better.

At the age of seven all slaves were put to work at something on the plantation, and Alick was no different. The work was hard and the hours were long, in the daylight and in the darkness. The slaves would get a little sleep and then be up before the sun to start it all again the next day.

Early in life Alick knew that this was not the way that he wanted to live. So in 1864, at the tender age of sixteen, Alick ran away from the plantation and joined the

45

Union army. He prayed long and hard that he would not get caught because he knew what they did to run away slaves. Alick used his slave experience to help himself in the army, he wasn't scared of hard work and always listened to those in authority. Soon after enlisting he was promoted to Sergeant of Company A.

After the Civil War Alick went to Texas and served as a Buffalo Soldier at Fort Concho, in San Angelo, Texas. He served as a Buffalo Soldier from 1873 until 1877. He fought in many battles against the Kickapoo, Comanche and Apache in the American-Indian War. While serving as a Buffalo Soldier Alick learned to both read and write. Soon he had made up his mind, he was going to return to Missouri and help his people to learn to read and write too. With his help maybe they too could become free peoples.

Alick came back to Missouri, with only this on his mind. He knew that he had to help the African Americans to learn so that they could survive as free people. He had $5,000 and was given another $1,500 for his project. Alick Bailey took this money and founded the Lincoln Institute, which is now known as Lincoln University in Jefferson City, Missouri.

Lincoln University is the only University founded by a Civil War Veteran, it is also the only University that was founded by and African American Veteran of any conflict. I think that history such as this is very important, for two main reasons. The first is so that we do not go back and repeat the bad history, and secondly so that we understand that we can overcome any hardship if we put our mind to it.

Unfortunately, I could not find the date of Alick's death or his place of burial. If anyone out there knows, then please call me with these details, as I am truly interested in how his story ended.

Great men are made by great dreams and small men are made by small dreams. So always dream big.

Ecclesiastes 9:10

"Whatever your hand finds to do, do it with your might; for there is no work or device or knowledge or wisdom in the grave where you are going."

Alick Bailey a runaway slave first sheriff of Lincoln County Missouri David Bailey

Norman McFadden

11

The Legend of Endless Love

The day was Thursday July 7th, 1877 and William Smith Sr. sat up from bed. He knew it was 5a.m. For the majority of his 78 years he had been getting up at 5a.m. Though his eyes were open he noticed that the light seemed dimmer than usual. He tried to rise from the bed, his trembling hand reaching for the bed post so he could pull himself upright. His head spinning as he stood and then walked over to the wash basin. The mirror showed him a man, withered and wrinkled from more than 50 years farming in the sun. Though he wasn't sure how much his hunched old body could bear.

He was used to it, living 78 years had brought him much pain and suffering. As he dressed, thoughts of his days in North Carolina kept running through his mind. In those days he could run a mile, but now just walking to the kitchen was almost more trouble than it was worth. His pushed his thoughts of younger days aside along with the pain. It was a new day and just like every one before it there were plenty of chores waiting to get done.

In the kitchen his wife Mary was setting the table, William stopped in the doorway just looking at her. Even after their many decades together, she was still just as beautiful as the day he'd married her. Through their hard years together and many children his love for her had not diminished one bit. Truthfully, he felt that he actually

49

loved her more every day. She looked up at him, "What are you gawking at?" "Only the most beautiful woman in the world." Was his reply. "Well, you just better eat your breakfast before it gets too cold." She told him with a smile.

"I love you now and forever." he said as he began eating. Mary walked over and kissed his forehead, and asked what he had planned for the day. He told her that since two of their sons were over helping the neighbor Captain Howell with his fields, that he would go down to their lower field and mend a broken fence and then head over to Capt. Howell's and maybe lend a hand. His wife asked him to be careful since he hadn't been feeling too well and that the temperature was over one hundred degrees.

William Smith Sr. reminded his wife that he loved her and headed out the door. Mary set herself to completing her own chores about the house. When lunch time came and went without any sign of William she began to worry, but had convinced herself that he was probably caught over at Captain Howell's, 'those two sure could yak up a storm', she told herself.

Around mid afternoon Mary went to rest in her rocking chair on the front porch, in no time she had fallen asleep. When she woke it was almost time for supper, she hurried into the house and cooked up a big meal knowing the men would be hungry after their day of hard work. The boys soon came home but William was not with them. When their mother asked they told her that they didn't know where their father was, that he had never made it next door.

The three rushed out of the house and down to the lower field, where he was going to work on the fence. As they approached they could see his cane hung on a cross beam and William sitting on the ground leaning on a fence post, his back toward them. As they came around, everyone knew that he was dead, his blank eyes staring into the evening sky. Mary fell to her knees beside her husband, she wept, but she knew that his pain would be no more. The boys recalled her saying, "You have left me, but your love is endless. In my heart you will never die."

Mr and Mrs. Smith lived in Lincoln County only four miles from Troy. They are buried side by side in Slavens Cemetery near Hawk Point, Missouri. Their endless love goes on.

1 Corinthians 13:1-13

"Though I speak with the tongues of men and of angels, but have not love, I have become sounding brass or a clanging cymbal. And though I have the gift of prophecy, and understand all mysteries and all knowledge, and though I have all faith, so that I could remove

51

mountains, but have not love, I am nothing. And though I bestow all my goods to feed the poor, and though I give my body to be burned, but have not love, it profits me nothing. Love suffers long and is kind; love does not envy; love does not parade itself, is not puffed up; does not behave rudely, does not seek its own, is not provoked, thinks no evil; does not rejoice in iniquity, but rejoices in the truth; bears all things, believes all things, hopes all things, endures all things. Love never fails. But whether there are prophecies, they will fail; whether there are tongues, they will cease; whether there *is* knowledge, it will vanish away. For we know in part and we prophesy in part. But when that which is perfect has come, then that which is in part will be done away. When I was a child, I spoke as a child, I understood as a child, I thought as a child; but when I became a man, I put away childish things. For now we see in a mirror, dimly, but then face to face. Now I know in part, but then I shall know just as I also am known. And now abide faith, hope, love, these three; but the greatest of these is love."

12

The Legend of John Hudson

Good Ole' John Hudson was born in North Carolina in 1796. But in 1819 he moved to Lincoln County with his dad, Isaac, when he was 22 years old. They settled in the Ninevah Township. Now Nineveh was the city in the Bible that Jonah didn't want to go to, the word Nineveh also meant unclean, it also was the name of a pagan goddess. But in this case it was simply Nineveh. Now you probably don't know Nineveh Township, but that is because in 1876 it became Olney and still is to this day.

Now Isaac Hudson was one of the earliest pioneers to settle in Lincoln County and he too was a well known man, having fought bravely in the Revolutionary War. Isaac was born in 1763 and passed away in 1848. When he moved to Missouri he was a blacksmith by trade.

John Hudson didn't follow his father's trade, he was a hunter and trapper. He spent most his time out in the woods and was hardly ever at home. Now he made good money trapping, but his home life was a mess. He went through three marriages and I guess after the third he had decided that he'd had enough, and he never did marry again.

It was maybe a year or so after John had moved to Lincoln County when it happened. John would remember it as the worst day of his life. It was a brutally cold December day with the wind blowing fiercely, the fine snow whipping around in the cold breeze occasionally making it impossible to see. John was packing up his trapping gear as his dad walked into the house, stomping the snow from his boots. Isaac dropped his load of wood next to the stove and looked his son over real good. Then immediately he set to trying to talk the young man into staying home.

While those who knew John might have said that he wasn't the 'sharpest tool in the shed' or that he 'wasn't much for talking' one thing they would have agreed on was that he was determined. He simply looked at his dad, picked up his hunting gear and headed out the door and straight over to the dog kennel. There he called out his two best dogs. From the way they were acting, they weren't too keen on an adventure in the back woods, but with a little encouragement they came along anyway.

There was a creek that ran along the north end of Nineveh Township, now John had never gone that far into the woods and trapped that creek, but he had heard that it was full of beaver. And he knew that beaver hide was easy to sell.

John set his mind on the trapping and pushed further into the woods. It wasn't like it is out there now, there was nothing for miles and miles but wilderness. It wasn't long before the wind began to blow harder, even taking John's hat and whisking it away into the increasing snow. It swirled between the trees and covered his tracks, when the wind blew the snow into his face John could hardly catch his breath. His dogs wouldn't even hunt now, they just huddled close to him as he walked.

The sun had set and John knew he had to do something to make a shelter and block the wind. He found himself a couple of good tree limbs and tried to make a lean-to with a quilt he had packed, but the wind quickly ripped it from his hands and blew it away.

Now he had no choice he had to find his way home, but which way was home. Every step only got him more lost, his feet were frozen, he didn't think his nose had ever been this cold and his ears felt as if they were going to just fall off. The thought of falling asleep and freezing to death was the only thing that kept him pushing forward, his feet getting heavier in the quickly deepening snow.

That was when it happened, he fell into a deep drift of snow and couldn't move. John just lay there looking at the sky, knowing that this was his last few moments alive. He later recounted the prayer that he said that night. "Lord, I'm not a church-goin' man, but I do believe. I can see your beauties all around me, You created all this by Your hands, the trees and leaves, flowers and bees, the stars You set in the sky, and the moon you have hung over our heads. I know in my heart that You exist. I ask you now if it's Your will to take me home, but if it's not would you please send me a miracle in the name of Jesus Christ. Amen."

John's eyes slowly closed as he finished his prayer, not knowing if he would ever see the sun rise again. But that night God did send a miracle. Somehow in the night John's two hunting dogs had dug out the snow all around him and cuddled as close as they could get to him. The warmth of the dog's fur had kept him alive, but sadly both of the dogs died. They had sacrificed their lives for his survival. From then on when he shut his eyes at night he could feel the arms of God wrapped tight around him and he knew that God still works miracles, because he was one.

Life is the most precious gift that God gives to us. Sometimes life is not so beautiful, but it is a beautiful life. When you are sitting around the Thanksgiving dinner table this year, look into the faces of your children, your grandchildren, your family and thank God for the precious gift of their life. This story is about someone that should have lost their life, but God decided to give them their life back with a miracle. I would like to wish you a very 'thankful for life' Thanksgiving.

Acts 4:30
"Stretch out your hand to heal and perform signs and wonders in the name of your holy servant Jesus."

13

The Legend of Pacing Diddle

Once in a lifetime God will send someone to you that will captivate your memory. From the first moment you meet them you know you will never forget them. Lincoln County had one of them people just about three miles from the little town of Troy. His nickname was Pacing Diddle, but his real name was Henry Overall.

He was born sometime around 1810 or so. No one seems to know the month though. Pacing Diddle was a black man and no one seemed to know his age. he was anywhere from 65 to 70 year old. he was a very unique man. He would gallup like a horse when he ran, and was said to be as fast as a horse too. He was a slave, owned by a Mr. W. Overall, who lived around Argentville, a small village about 15 miles north east of Troy Missouri.

When he was freed, and no longer a slave, he moved to a small settlement of black people about 2 miles northeast of Troy, called Needmore. He carried the name of Henry Overall, but went by Pacing Diddle. He had three daughters, Susie, Ellen, and Mary. Pacing Diddle would come to town every Saturday. He would carry a short whip and whip his legs when he wanted to go faster.

He would carry a small sack over his shoulder to carry stuff back from Troy for people who couldn't make the trip for themselves. He never simply walked, he always moved at a fast pace, swinging his legs from one side to the other like a horse, throwing up a cloud of dust as he went.

Another thing that made him so unique, was how he would put his hands under his armpits and flap his arms like wings, and crow like a rooster. The children of Troy were terrified of Pacing Diddle, and the mothers didn't help anything by telling scary stories of Pacing Diddle to them.

Mothers gave children warnings like "If you don't come in at night, Pacing Diddle will get you. He can leap right over a fence without touching it with his hands." The children knew that he could run faster than a horse and that no one would get away if he wanted them!

"These were only made up stories just to scare the kids though. He was actually a real good man, even if he was very different. Sometimes in the world if you're just a little different you're not accepted. Just to prove how fast he really was, I'm going to tell you a little story.

He had a race with a man on a horse, the man's name was Dr. Wardie, a doctor in the town of Troy at that time. Pacing Diddle had to make the race on foot. The distance was like 17 miles across the countryside. The race was in the hottest part of the summer, in July. In the beginning of the race, the doctor took off fast and had about a mile lead advantage. About halfway through the race the doctor's horse got overheated and fell dead. Pacing Diddle ran on and finish the race. Then he went back to where the doctor's horse had fell dead.

There he picked up the saddle and carried it on his back to Troy. The next amazing thing that Pacing Diddle did, was he trotted all the way to St Louis and he ran into someone he knew from Troy. The person that he ran into was Mr Walt Perkins, and Walt was riding his horse.

He had heard about the race that Pacing Diddle had with Dr. Wardie. So Mr. Perkins challenged Pacing Diddle to a race back to Troy. Before they took off Diddle asked Mr Perkins, "Is there anything you want me to tell you wife when I get there?" Mr. Perkins said replied; "What are you talking about? I'm riding a horse and you are on foot." Then with a laugh, he said, "Tell her to have supper ready when I get there." Diddle said "Okay." and off he went!

By the time Mr Perkins got home around midnight, his wife did have supper on the table. Pacing Diddle had already told her, and was back at his house. It was 55 miles from St. Louis to Troy and he beat a man on a horse.

The listing of his death was July 25th, 1890. A black male body, probably around 80 years of age, was found in the quiver river bottoms. They said the body was none other than Henry Overall (Pacing Diddle). This man was truly amazing. But most people back in them days didn't realize just how amazing he really was.

Isaiah 40:31

"But those who hope in the Lord will renew their strength. They will soar on wings like eagles, they will run and not grow weary, they will walk and not be faint."

2 Timothy 4:7

"I have fought a good fight, I have finished the race, I have kept the faith."

Norman McFadden

14

The Legend of the Slicker War

This is a war that most people have never heard of. But it actually happened and many innocent people lost their lives. It happened because certain people thought that they were above the law, and they started taking the law into their own hands. Back in the year 1840 the Slicker War began in Benton and Polk Counties. That war was much like what happened between the Hatfield's and McCoy's. It truly began because of one family not liking another family.

Now let me begin by explaining what exactly a 'slicker' was. A slicker was a person who decided that the were judge, jury and executioner all in one. If they thought someone was guilty of a crime, well they would get right to slicking the guilty party. Now 'slicking' is a backwoods slang term for whipping. The slickers were known tit the guilty person to a tree then take a green oak switch and beat the person until they were half dead, or worse. Sometimes they would shoot the person after the beating, other times the person would just vanish. The slickers were also known to tell people to get out of the county by a certain time, and if you were seen again after that time you were shot on sight.

Soon this violence had spread to Lincoln County. About half of the residents were for the slickers, but the other half were not. But in Lincoln County it started for what seemed like a good reason, at the time there were rustlers out here stealing cows, pigs and horses. The Slicker War truly began in Lincoln County, Missouri in 1843 and went until 1845.

Mr. James Stallard of Hurricane Township was elected captain of all the slickers. (Lincoln County's slickers were a little more organized than those in Benton and Polk Counties.) At the beginning they operated more like a business than vigilantes. Mr. Stallard had Brice Hammock draw up a contract and bylaws for each of the slickers to sign and agree to. But just like with anything else, when a man gets too much power it goes to his head.

In Lincoln County the slickers were the cream of the crop. They were well known men in the area. Men like Ira T. Nelson, Rolla Mayer, Abraham and Joshua King, Rufus Gibson and many others. They were the richest and most powerful men in the county. Now these were not only the most well known men in the county, but now they had real power in their hands. And they decided to wield that power. They started deciding who would be allowed to live in Lincoln County and who was going to have to go. Some used their position to settle personal grudges. It didn't take long for what had started off as a good thing to quickly turn bad.

Someone in the Slickers decided that they did not like John Plummer, so he in turn made up a tale and told it to the other Slickers about John being a horse thief. When the Slickers met to discuss what to do about John Plummer they thought that maybe it would be better since he had a very nice piece of property to run him out of the county rather than whipping him. Well John wasn't about to pick up his family and abandon everything that he had. On the day that John was supposed to be out of the county he was seen in Troy buying a few things. On his way home he was bushwhacked by several men and shot dead. This did not sit well with some of the people in Lincoln County, and the Slickers began to lose some of their support.

Then came someone accusing one of James Turnbull's sons of horse theft. But this was a lie told by someone who simply disliked the man. But the Slickers acted on it anyway. The gave the man a date to be gone, but he also disobeyed. The attack on the Turnbull homestead immediately followed. Reports say that it was a terrible slaughter. With multiple people shot or stabbed there were deaths and miraculous recoveries on both sides.

The Assault on the Turnbull house was the last straw for people in St. Charles County who wanted none of this nonsense around their homes. In Flint Hill a group formed calling themselves the Anti-Slickers. They made it their duty to put a stop to the Slickers once and for all. The war between the two parties lasted for almost a full year. For one reason or another people began to lose interest in the fight and left on their separate ways. In 1845 both parties disbanded and things went back to normal. Now that is what you would call vigilante justice on the frontier.

1 Peter 2:13-17

"Submit yourselves to every ordinance of man for the Lord's sake: whether it be to the king, as supreme; Or unto governors, as unto them that are sent by him for the punishment of evildoers, and for the praise of them that do well. For so is the will of God, that with well doing ye may put to silence the ignorance of foolish men: As free, and not using your liberty for a cloak of maliciousness, but as the servants of God. Honor all men. Love the brotherhood. Fear God. Honor the king."

15

The Lincoln County Gunfight

Lincoln County, Missouri, is right near the heart of the Gateway to the West. Back in 1868, gun slinging Cowboys were everywhere. And Lincoln County was no different. It was a cold day on November 12, the wind was blowing from the north, and it would chill a man to his bones.

The story takes place in a little town in Lincoln County called Chantilly, Missouri. Chantilly was laid out in 1852 and named after Chantilly in French. A post office was set up in 1840 and it was in operation until 1918. I drove out to the little town, but there is nothing there that you can see from the naked eye.

But you can feel the spirits stirring, the old gun fights back in the days when everyone packed a gun on his hip. John Freeland Rose got up just like any other day, he was a 23 year old young man. He went to work that morning and worked till around three in the afternoon. It seemed like any other day, but this day was not going to be like any other day at all.

He got off work and decided to go to Chantilly and talk to some friends of his. They all like gathering on the street to talk and just have fun. So he left work on his horse and rode over to visit with his friends in the small town. As he arrived he saw a group of friends standing on the street corner, so he went over to join them.

As he stood there talking, from the side, Jessie Bray walked up. Without saying a word he drew his gun from his holster and shot young John Ross without saying a word. The bullet went into John's stomach and he fell to the ground. Jessie ran off the moment he was shot, and John's friends fired several shots at Jesse as he ran off.

Apparently they weren't good shots, because they missed him. He ducked in some bushes and escaped. Hearsay was that Jessie had something against John's older brother Captain Thomas Rose, that happened over in Quincy, Illinois the year before. And a couple of weeks before the shooting, they had words which almost came to blows. As the smoke from the pistols filled the air, they picked up young John's bleeding limp body. They carried John to the nearest doctor. He died the next day. On that cold November day in 1868, John Freeland Rose lost his life at the age of 23.

Genesis 4:9;
"Then the Lord said to Cain, "Where is your brother able?" "I do not know," replied Cain. "Am I My Brother's Keeper?"

16

The Lincoln County Outlaw Gang

Who in Missouri has not heard of Jesse James? Jesse James was the famous Outlaw leader of the James Gang back in the 1800's. But there was another outlaw gang that popped up at the same time, right here in Lincoln County, Missouri. Everything that happened to him was similar to what happened to Jesse James. The were alike in many ways.

They both fought for the Confederate side. They both had their houses burned down. And they both were leaders of outlaw gangs. This is the story of Captain Thomas Benton Rose. He was born right here in Troy, Missouri, in 1837. His dad was Freeland W. Rose, and his mom was Mary Rose. Thomas helped his dad on the farm here in Lincoln County. He got married to Laura J. Cassidy and started having kids.

His life was pretty good until he turned 23. from there it was all downhill for Thomas. About that time he got into a personal dispute with a man by the name of Creed. Back in them days the Creed family was a pretty powerful family. Thomas was arrested by the militia and placed in prison. Then he got out of prison about a year later. It seemed like he just couldn't get along well here in Lincoln County.

So Thomas packed up everything and moved to Arkansas. There he joined the Confederate Army in 1861. After serving three years he came out as a captain in 1864. He loaded up his family and moved back to Lincoln County. He thought in his mind that everything would be over and he could have a good life in Lincoln County again. But it wasn't a couple of months after he came back that the Militia burned down his house. That was the straw that broke the camel's back.

He went out and rounded up a bunch of Army buddies and friends to join his gang. Thomas started sneaking across the Mississippi River into Illinois to steal and murder. From August of that year to the following May, he got away with it. But on May 31, his luck ran out.

There was a policeman in Chicago that was a confederate sympathizer. He helped Captain Rose and his gang get back and forth across the Mississippi River. On May 31, the policeman played the double cross. Rose wrote him and told him where he was and said he needed some extra men to help him rob a bank. But instead of helping him, the policeman told the other authorities where Captain Rose and his men were staying out on a farm.

So the authorities got a posse together and raided the farm. During the shootout at the farm, Captain Ross took two shots, one in his chest, and one to the stomach.

As a result of his gunshot wounds, he was captured. They captured two of his men also, a 16 year old named Quincy Ben, and Charles Barnascone.

The other members of the gang got away. They were all three taken to the Adams County Jail in Quincy Illinois. They didn't think captain Ross would make it through the night with his wounds. But that night a Lynch Mob, around 500 in all citizens and army got together and surrounded the jail house. They were screaming and hollering with torches lit, demanding that the sheriff bring Captain Rose out. The sheriff refused, and the angry mob started jumping over the fence into the courtyard.

Using a sledgehammer, they broke down the jailhouse door. As they brought Rose out. He was drenched in his own blood from his wounds. They dragged him for a mile to the hanging tree. As they threw him on the ground below the tree, Captain Rose cried out for someone to pray for him. A man came from the crowd and said he would pray for him. After the prayer a reporter asked if he could talk to Ross. the Lynch Mob was in a hurry to hang him, but they said he could have a minute. The reporter said that he had a military hat and his shirt was ripped down the front and blood was coming from his wounds. He had no shoes on, and his toes were sticking out from his wore out socks. His eyes were almost swollen shut from the beating that the lynch Mob had given him on the way to the tree. His mouth was swollen and bleeding. he didn't have the strength to stand.

These are Captain Thomas Benton Rose's last words on May 31, 1865, at approximately 11p.m.

"I live near Troy in Lincoln County, Missouri, have a wife and three children living there now. In 1860 I voted for Stephen A. Douglas for president, John B. Henderson for Congress. About that time I got in a personal dispute with a man by the name of Creed. But through his influence I was arrested by the militia and placed in prison. I stayed a long while. My house was burnt by the militia in August, so I went to Arkansas, and was commissioned by Kirby Smith as a captain in the Confederate Army."

The mob wouldn't let him talk any longer. They were in a hurry to Hang him. They stacked some wooden boxes up for his feet to stand on. They threw a rope over the limb on the hanging tree, and slipped it around his neck. and with that they kicked the boxes out from under his feet. No one got in trouble for the hanging of Captain Thomas Benton Rose at the age of 27.

Hosea 4:2

"There is only cursing, lying and murder, and adultery, They break all bounds, and Bloodshed follows bloodshed."

17

The Millwood School House

One room schoolhouses have fallen by the wayside, much like dreams that seem to fade away as smoke in the wind. But to lose all memory of yesterday would be like losing our dreams of tomorrow. Most children these days have never seen or even heard of a one room schoolhouse, with only one teacher teaching thirty to forty students everything from first all the way up to eighth grade.

In my writing I have traveled to many little towns along the back-roads of Missouri. I have talked to many people and I take them all to heart. I feel their pain, sorrow and happiness. I stop in these little towns that are just not what they used to be. Millwood, Missouri is one of the back road towns. The small town seems to fade just like the sun does as the darkness takes the light away. These little towns almost seem as if there is a dark cloud from the past that just hangs over them. The thought of towns such as these fading into nothing but memory actually brings tears to my eyes.

So in my driving I stopped in the town of Millwood. I went into the beauty shop that still clings to life in the forgotten town. I struck up a conversation with the lovely lady that owns the shop. Her name is Janis Hurt and she told me about a little one room school that sits out on a farm on Highway D.

Now my first years of school were spent in a tiny one room schoolhouse down in Leeper, Missouri and this certainly piqued my curiosity. Well, I headed right out to Highway D about four miles south of Millwood. As I turned onto the state highway it was right there on my left. A one room school shining like a beacon from the past! It is sitting out on Mr. Jim Mudd's farm. He had moved it from the original location and has restored it to it's original beauty.

The elite people of Lincoln County had graduated from that school just as had the earlier generations of the Mudd family. Doctors, judges, lawyers and even poets and authors had walked through that tiny schoolhouse when they were children..

The schoolhouse was named after the Reddish family, on whose property it sat. The Reddish family all went to that tiny schoolhouse. Mr. William H. Reddish was born on September 28th, 1846 in Millwood, Missouri. He had six children before he passed away at the young age of thirty-five in May of 1881, also in Millwood, Missouri. He was laid to rest in the old Liberty Cemetery in Millwood.

Mr. Jim Mudd was kind enough to come and open the doors and let me see the inside of that incredible one room school. I took a few more pictures than I normally would have because I want to share the beauty of it with you. I want you to feel what I felt when I looked inside. It took me back to my childhood as I walked through those doors.

As I walked down the front hall the lunch buckets hung neatly on their hooks, then into the main classroom. To my left was a little case with the first aid supplies and then on my right was a big glass case with all kinds of old books and school items, sitting on top was a guest book for the visitors to sign. I was quite proud to sign my name in that little booklet.

The seats were arranged by size starting with the small desks and on to the larger ones, a huge chalkboard stretched from one end of the classroom to the other. And the teacher's desk sat at the front where he or she would sit and teach the children. You would have to see it to understand just how beautiful it is.

It reminded me of a beautiful flower that had been plucked in full bloom, but now it had lost all it's lovely petals and faded away. It took me back to a time when things were much simpler. But to get to the point, it simply took my breath away.

Can you just imagine eight classes and one teacher. You wouldn't think that the teacher would have time for one-on-one with the students, but they did. As time goes by many people think that things are getting better, but I have to ask myself, 'Are they?'. Time has passed the one room schoolhouse by. And the large towns of the 1800's are now almost ghost towns. Sometimes I find myself looking at a stronger town and wishing to have seen it in its full glory. But they are just drying up and blowing away. It brought a tear to my eye. Is it better? This reporter didn't really think so. (I think we need to look back to see where we came from to know where we are going. Focus on the mistakes that they made in time gone by so we don't end up making the same mistakes again.)

As I travel the back roads of Lincoln County I can feel the rich history that lies in each small town and a sense of pride in the people who have stayed. Why don't you get in the car one of these Sundays and take a visit to these small towns and let it run through your mind about what they used to be. Listen to me folks, these small towns are the heart of our county.

2 Peter 1:12

"Wherefore I will not be negligent to put you always in remembrance of these things, though ye know them, and be established in the present truth."

18

The Moscow Mills Bridge

I was sitting at home one day on my deck watching the rabbits play in the yard. That is what I do when I'm not writing. I was just looking at how beautiful nature is, and how blessed we are with all the things that God has given us. But why is it sometimes that human nature causes us to take things that are beautiful and tear them up and trash them. The story at hand came about when a lady called me very disturbed about a certain place in Lincoln County. She said that it has been overrun by drug dealers and users. She told me that her name is Cheryl, but that she did not want her last name mentioned because of the fear of retaliation. She brought me this tip and even helped me to get interviews with some of the people. Thank you, Cheryl, very much for your help.

It is time for the good people of Lincoln County to rise up. There is a place out here that is known for drug trafficking. This is a place where people have drowned, committed suicide, and even recently emergency vehicles had to be brought in to rescue two children who were in danger. These people are dying and their blood is crying up from the ground. These are needless deaths that, as good citizens, we should take an interest in doing something about.

These things go on right under our noses, and we go on playing a little game with it. That game is called 'ignore it and it will go away'. Give me a break! It's not going to go away, not unless the good people of Lincoln County put their collective foot down and say 'We are not going to tolerate this anymore'. We need to band together and run the drug dealers out of that area, and then do something to improve it. Right now it is an accident waiting to happen. Neighbors in that area have contacted me and asked if I could write an article about this place. I went out and did much investigating, and I found out that everything that they were telling me is true. In my lifetime I have learned that the statement is true, 'evil only wins when good people do nothing'.

To let you know, I am talking about the old Moscow Mills bridge. The old bridge was built in 1885 by Raymond and Campbell. It was originally fabricated by Carnegie Stell and later erected by Raymond and Campbell. It was the first all metal span across the Cuivre River in Lincoln County. The Moscow Mills bridge was later damage by heavy flood waters in the winter of 1890. The riverbank was also washed away around the bridge, resulting in it needing extensive repair work. Over time the bridge became an eyesore in the community.

But now it is worse than an eyesore and Lincoln County needs to take action before something serious happens. One neighbor told me that he woke up one morning to find a man suffering from a heroin overdose in his driveway. Another said that they were watching TV one day when they started hearing children screaming. They went outside to see two children hanging off the bridge crying for help. Another yet told me that there have been multiple suicides and at least one accidental drowning.

Everyone in the area will agree that all you have to do is go outside and walk the streets for a few minutes and you will find used drug needles. Tennis shoes hanging over the power lines typically means that this is a place for drug deals, well they are all over down by the bridge and I have the pictures to prove it.

What are we going to do about this? Are we going to sit on our butts and let it continue to happen or get out there and do something about it? I have been studying local Lincoln County history for many years and we are not the type of people to let this happen. We are the type of people that get things done.

Ephesians 6:10 -20

"Find his strength in the Lord and in his mighty power. Put on the full armor of God. So that you can take on your Stand against the devil's schemes. For our struggle if not against the flesh and blood, but against the rulers, against the authorities, against the power of this dark world and against the spiritual forces of evil in the heavens realms. Therefore put on the full armor of God, so that when the day of evil comes you may be able to stand your ground, and after you have done everything to stand, stand firm then with the belt of truth, buckle around your waist, with the breastplate of righteousness in place, and with your feet filled with the readiness that come from the gospel of peace."

Norman McFadden

19

The Old Monroe Bank Robbery

It was a brazen daylight robbery! it was like a combination of Bonnie and Clyde and a little bit of The Three Stooges all mixed up in one. It involved both greed, and a lot of stupidity.

It was a hot summer day in 1935. The wind was blowing in lightly from the southeast. Three men driving cross-country in a vehicle that they had stolen. They stopped in St. Charles to get a bite of food. They were getting low on money, but they didn't want to take a chance of robbing any location in a big city.

It was morning when they left St. Charles, Missouri. They had no idea where they were going, or what they were going to do. They headed north on Highway 79 and they came upon the little town of Old Monroe, Missouri. They had no plans at all, it was just a spur of the moment thing.

They figured that there would be less police officers in a small town, so as the three drove into Old Monroe they set their sights on a little small town bank. They didn't figure a town this small would even have a bank. They were going to rob a little general store or something. The leader of the group was about as dumb as a box of rocks. The other two were lower down on the totem pole than he was when it came to common horse sense.

It was around 11 a.m. when they walked into the bank of Old Monroe. They all three had guns and they were just stupid enough to use them. When they came into the bank they were friendly, talking to everyone with big smiles across their faces. They thought their smiles would cover up the dirty evil plot that was raging in their minds.

No one expected a thing! They just seemed like three friendly fellows that had come in off the street to do some banking. They were going to do some banking alright, they were planning on making a large withdrawal. They kind of waited around a little bit until the bank cleared out. That was when they drew their guns, and told everyone to lay on the floor, and lock their hands behind their backs.

They made Mr. Ed Goss get up off of the floor, despite his protesting every minute of it. They handed him bags, and told him to go to all the cash drawers and fill the bags full of money. The youngest one looked out the window and saw a crowd of people gathering in the streets. He thought for sure that their cover had been blown.

But a matter of fact it was just people talking as they congregated in front of the bank. They knew nothing about the robbery. But through his stupidity, the young robber informed the leader that there was a large group coming for them. The robbers suddenly expected to be ambushed and killed.

The leader of the three said "We will take us a hostage." It seemed to be a good decision. After Ed filled all the bags full of money, They got Blanche Hemmersmeyer from the bank floor. They put both of the hostages, Ed and Blanche, in front of them as they walked out the door, got into their vehicle and drove away.

The people in the street had no idea of what was going on. Not a shot was fired! They dropped off the two hostages at the edge of town unharmed. The men got away with $561.00. I could not find a report on whether or not they ever got caught.

It was a daring robbery in the middle of the day in Old Monroe, Missouri, in the summer of 1935. The bank of Old Monroe was established in 1906. They built a new bank in the same location in 1960. I tried my best to find out what the three robbers names were, and where they were from. But I had no success at finding out. After many interviews with local folks, this was all the information I got.

Ephesians 4:28

"Let a thief no longer steal, but rather let him labor, doing honest work with his hands, so he may have something to share with everyone in need."

Norman McFadden

20

The Screaming House

There are some weird legends about houses that sit out in the woods. This legend is about a house that sits up on a big hill overlooking a spooky looking holler full of trees. The legend has it that the big two-story white house was occupied by an old lady and old man who lived there with their daughter until they died.

The daughter had some mental problems that she dealt with. She weighed around 200 pounds and walked with a little limp and used a cane. After her mom and dad died she lived in this big old house by herself. Everyone around that neck of the woods knew she was all alone by herself in the house. A man from a nearby town thought she would be easy prey. So he decided he was going to go up there and pay a visit to Rosemary.

He got there around 11 p.m. and busted through the door. Once he was in the house he chased Rosemary to the bedroom upstairs and raped her. The police caught him about a week later. He got 5 years in prison, but that did not do Rosemary any good. She became pregnant, and being weak of mind, she didn't really understand what was going on.

Nine months later Rosemary had a healthy little girl. After the baby was born she was confused about how to take care of the baby when it cried. She put the baby's crib in her bedroom upstairs. The exact same room that she was raped in. But nobody offered to help poor Rosemary with the baby.

People say that at night she would scream so loud that it would echo up and down the holler all night long. When the baby was crying Rosemary's agonizing scream could be heard for miles. One night it all came to a boiling Point. Rosemary couldn't take it anymore and lost her mind completely. The little baby was only three weeks old. Rosemary started screaming at the baby "what's wrong with you? Please stop crying."

You have to understand that Rosemary was 35 but had the mind of a 10 year old. She did not understand why the baby just kept crying. Rosemary said that she had all she could take and couldn't take any more. She picked up the baby, kissed it on the cheek, and then opened the second floor window. She Threw the baby from the window to the unforgiving hard concrete that lay below.

You could hear the baby crying all the way down. Then the baby stopped crying. Rosemary took a look at her little baby girl laying on the concrete. She leaped from the same window, and screamed all the way down until she smashed onto the concrete with her head. Then the screaming stopped altogether.

They say that every night the baby will cry and Rosemary will scream. And it won't stop until you hear the smack on the concrete.

Ask yourself, is death the end or is it just the beginning? If it is the beginning, what is it the beginning of? Myself, I think it's the beginning of what you created for yourself while you were here on Earth. But back to the story.

They say that nobody can stay all night in that house, because a lot a people have tried. I contacted the owner and asked if I could stay the night in the house. He gave me permission under one circumstance; that I could not reveal the location of the house to anyone. However, I can reveal it is in Lincoln County, Missouri. I couldn't help but think that this house is what nightmares are made of.

On March 6, I made it out to the screaming house around 4pm. I parked my car at the bottom of the hill, and made my way up the hill to the big rusty metal fence that surrounded the yard of the house. As I opened the metal gate it let out an awful squeak. As I passed through the gate I was looking up at that big two-story house with the paint peeling off of every side. From the yard I could sense the evil that lived in that house.

The thought ran through my head, 'This is going to be the last night of my life. Am I going to be able to stay all night in the screaming house?'. I walked up the stairs to the front of the house. As I stuck the key into the front door lock, and slowly opened it, I could feel the cold wind on my back. Which made the hair raise up on the back of my neck.

I have got to say that I don't really believe in ghosts, but there are some things in this world that we cannot explain. 'Is this going to be one of the nights that I can't explain what has happened?', I wondered. In my mind I was thinking that I should have brought someone with me just in case. It was cloudy all day but the moment I walked in the house I heard the thunder. I was in for a stormy night on top of a spooky hill, in a scary haunted house.

'Give me a break!', I thought, As I settled in for the night. As I was unpacking my backpack I noticed that I had forgotten my anointing oil to bless the windows and the doors. I thought in my mind, 'This is going to be one of those crazy nights.'. I still went and prayed over every window, and every doorway without the anointing oil. It took quite a while because there were many windows and doorways.

I decided to stay in the downstairs because the violent incidents happened upstairs. The house was really dusty and there were cobwebs hanging from every part of the ceiling in the house. I laid my blanket down on the floor, because I wasn't about to sleep on any of the furniture that was in there. I took my thermos and my beef jerky out of my backpack and proceeded to eat and drink. The rain was making a tapping noise up on the tin roof. The thunder was so loud it shook the house, as the lightning lit up the sky through the open windows.

After I finished eating I retrieved my flashlight and my Bible from the backpack. I began to read scriptures from the holy word of God. It was around 11 p.m. when I heard something upstairs pacing back and forth across the floor. It sounded like someone heavy and walking with a cane. I could hear the footsteps and the cane; click, click, click, on the floor.

Then I heard a crying sound, like a baby. I thought in my mind that it could have been the howling of the wind through a window upstairs. Because the wind was blowing real hard outside. As the pacing got louder and louder and the tapping of the cane on the floor continued, I started to get a little bit on the nervous side. As a matter of fact, I was as nervous as a long-tailed cat in a room full of rocking chairs.

Then it happened; a scream burst out that sounded like a woman who was being hurt. Her voice was saying, 'Stop crying'. I decided to get up and walk up the stairs to the second floor. With flashlight in hand I slowly walked up the staircase. There were two bedrooms upstairs. I looked in one, but saw nothing. I walked in the other one next and saw nothing.

I went back downstairs. The moment I sat on the blanket I heard something like a baby crying and a woman screaming again, and then the window opened up. Suddenly there were sounds of a long cry outside from the upstairs falling to the concrete and then it stopped. And then I heard something like woman scream a long scream from the upstairs window to the concrete. Then I heard it no more all night.

It was quiet. I don't know what I heard that night, but I did stay all night. I don't know if it was a wind blowing through the upstairs window or down the chimney. Maybe it was just my imagination? Make up your mind for yourself. Is the legend of the screaming house true or false? In my eyes it happened, and the restless spirits are still there. It is most certain that we all will die, but when we die our spirits will be with the Lord. But every person carries other spirits within them. And upon death they come out looking for other hosts.

2 Corinthians 5:8;
"We are confident, yes, well pleased rather to be absent from the body, and to be present with the Lord."

21

The Weeping Lady

First I will let you know that I have no intention of offending anyone, and since there may still be family living in Lincoln County, I have been asked to change the names so that they may remain private. I am going to tell you this legend exactly as it was told to me.

Miss Joan was born in Lincoln County, North Carolina in 1815. When she was only three years old her family moved to Lincoln County, Missouri. They arrived at Clark's Fort, now named Moscow Mills, in June of 1818. From there they purchased some land and moved to a hilltop overlooking Crooked Creek, only six miles outside of Troy, Missouri.

Miss Joan's childhood passed and as a young woman she married a war hero, named Thomas, who had served with Stonewall Jackson during the Civil War. They had been married for a few years when Joan finally got pregnant. Sadly this was when poor Joan's life was turned upside down. On July first, 1833 Joan gave birth to a beautiful baby girl they named Emily. Emily was a lovely child, but at only thirteen months old on August seventh of 1834 little Emily died. There was no known cause of death. Joan wept and cried out to God as she walked the narrow pathway from their house to the small graveyard, all dressed in black. She watched as her baby was buried, her hand on her belly as she knew that she was with child again.

December fourth, 1834 she went into labor, but the baby was stillborn. Though it was a brutally cold day with snow on the ground, Thomas went out to the graveyard and began to dig the tiny grave. As they carried Mary's small body down the narrow pathway, Joan clothed all in black once again wept and cried out, her veil covering her face and her long black dress whipping in the winter wind. With her second child laid to rest, she fell to the ground and cried out to God, 'Why have You cursed my family?'.

Time passed and Joan became pregnant yet again. November twenty-first 1836 Joan gave birth to a beautiful, bouncing, baby boy, they named him James. James thrived and for the next ten years Thomas and Joan did not know if she would ever bear again. But with having lost two children Joan wanted nothing more than to have another baby to hold in her arms.

To everyone's surprise Joan did conceive again. On November nineteenth, 1846 little Elizabeth was born. Now Joan and Thomas had two healthy children and two who had never even lived long enough to know what life was about. If only they had stopped there. In March of 1853 Joan gets pregnant a fifth time, and the tragedy continued.

The day before Christmas, December twenty fourth, 1853 Joan gave birth to a sweet baby boy they named John. But during the labor Joan began to bleed, by the time the flow stopped she had lost a huge amount of blood, but managed to survive. Throughout the cold, hard winter she became weaker and weaker. The following summer came quickly with drought and high temps. The last year of Joan's life she seemed as a withered old lady. On August seventh, 1854, at the age of 39, Joan succumbed and breathed her last breath and moved on to whatever the afterlife held for her.

Unfortunately, though Joan had passed her suffering continued. One his first birthday, December twenty-fourth, 1854, what should have been celebration was replaced with tragedy when John suddenly passed away. They said that you could hear Joan's wailing cries as they carried his small body to the graveyard that held the children. As he heard the cries of his deceased wife, Thomas fell to his knees calling out to God, asking why He had cursed his family.

The legend says that on the anniversary of each of her children's deaths that you can hear her cries carrying up the valley and along the small pathway that led from their home to the graveyard. And if you watch you just may catch a glimpse of the Weeping Lady, dressed all in black as the wind whips her dress and veil while she stands atop the hill overlooking Crooked Creek.

As a Christian I know that God does not curse people and He also does not tempt them. But God will allow them to be tested.

Job 3:20-26

"Wherefore is light given to him that is in misery, and life unto the bitter in soul; Which long for death, but it comes not; and dig for it more than for hid treasures. Which rejoice exceedingly, and are glad, when they can find the grave? Why is light given to a man whose way is hid, and whom God hath hedged in? For my sighing comes before I eat, and my roarings are poured out like the waters. For the thing which I greatly feared is come upon me, and that which I was afraid of is come unto me.

I was not in safety, neither had I rest, neither was I quiet; yet trouble came."

22

The White Swan School House

Time goes by so quickly, just as a fluffy white cloud floating across the sky. One moment it is there and the next it is gone. When you are on the hilltop life looks so exciting, but when you are halfway down you simply long to be back at the top. We cannot forget where we came from and the mistakes that we have made in the past. Otherwise we would just end up making the same mistakes over and over again.

If you would like to climb to the top again, grab that puffy cloud and drag it back, or perhaps just go back in time for only a day, then I suggest you take a drive out State Hwy F in Eolia, Missouri. Ride out there and visit Mark and Patty Koenig on their farm. I am sure they will welcome you with open arms, just as they did me.

Out there, one the far edge of Lincoln County, sitting out in the field are three log cabins decorated just as they would have been back in the 1800's. And rising from the ground like a white ghost is the White Swan one room Schoolhouse. I researched and was able to find documents dating the school to 1898.

Many families from Lincoln County, Missouri went to that one room schoolhouse. Though I am not from one of those families that graduates from there. A few names you might know would be the Potts, Blackwell, Brown, Briggs, Davis, Watt and Springston families. There are so many more families that just these few which I have named here.

There were so many things there that I had never seen before in the cabins. Then Patty and I drove across the field to the School, stepping into the front door took me back to that hilltop of my child hood. It reminded me of a time when life was so good and I felt so young again that I never wanted to leave.

The seats were lined up on each side of the school, and in the middle was an old wood-burning stove. The teacher's desk was sitting up front with the chalkboard and a little stage right behind it. Just for old times sake I had to sit at one of the student's desk and drift back to when I was six years old sitting in that little one-room schoolhouse in southern Missouri.

Lift your heart and feel young again. Go out and visit Patty and Mark. Go back in time to the 1800's, it'll be a short trip, but it might be the long journey back into your childhood that you need.

Psalm 90:12;
"So teach us to number our days, that we may gain a heart of wisdom."

Norman McFadden

23

The Legend of Auburn, Missouri 1

AUBURN SCHOOL NOV. 6, 1899

During the Indian Uprising of 1812 the army built a fort just north of a spring in Lincoln County, Missouri. This fort was named Stout's Fort. A small town began to grow around the fort and the eastern part became known as Auburn, named after Auburn, New York. In 1838 the United States Postal Service opened up a Post office and the settlement officially became a town.

The very first doctor in the town was Daniel Draper Sr. and then after him came Dr. William McClurd. The first Justice of the Peace was James Wilson, who also performed the first Auburn wedding between Hiram McDonald and Eliza Ann Tilford. There was a cotton gin just a little ways out of town, which was run by Vivian Thacker.

A short line railroad ran from Bellflower, Missouri to Troy, Missouri with a stop in Auburn between the two. This made easy travel for people who wanted to do business in Troy. They could catch the train into Troy, conduct their business and then ride the train home when it returned in the morning. This was certainly safer and easier than riding horses of wagons the fair distance.

By 1888 a general store had been added, Jim Terre ran the store and the Post Office. A full-time blacksmith shop was owned by C. Teague, and a Presbyterian Church had been built. At this time Joseph A. Knox was the local doctor. A one room school-house had been built and many of Lincoln County's elite citizens had attended that school. It was even believed that there were as many as a hundred people living in Auburn at the time. It was some time later when they constructed a hotel right in the heart of the town.

There are two graveyards in Auburn, one right near the town's center and the second is a small family graveyard a half mile south. It is the Cochran family graveyard, laid to rest there are 8 Cochrans, 1 Knox and 1 Weems.

Maybe next month I will share with you the story of the Cochran family. They only lived a short way from the family graveyard. Like most families they had their black sheep. But this family had not one, but two wild ones. There were two brothers that were always stirring up some trouble and were always standing right in the middle of it. These brothers did not let any one walk on them or their family. George and John Cochran said what they meant and meant what they said. During their time they ran the store in fort, but if you walked into that store you had better have been nice.

Psalm 27:1

"The Lord is my light and my salvation; Whom should I fear? The Lord is the strength of my life; of whom shall I be afraid?"

Norman McFadden

24

The Legend of Auburn, Missouri 2

In the small town of Auburn, Missouri, just outside of Stout's Fort, was what some people called the best General Store in all of Lincoln County. In 1875 it was ran by the Cochran brothers, Andrew, George and John. Now Andrew was the kind of man that never found trouble, but George and John were wild. I fell that I am a little like they were, as they were always ready to stand up for their family and to fight for their town and neighbors, but sometimes they sure went about it the wrong way.

In 1875 a man named James M. Teagus stole a horse from one of the Cochran brother's neighbors. Mr. Teagus had already served time in the state penitentiary for previous crimes that he had committed. This time when he was caught James Teagus was to stand trial in Auburn, Missouri, but they only had a Justice of the Peace. Mr. Teagus refused to be tried by anyone less than a judge, so he would have to be transported to Troy to have his trial by judge there.

The Cochran brothers felt that this was an insult to their community. They said that since he had committed the crime in Auburn, then he should be tried in Auburn, and they devised a plan. The day for Mr. Teagus to be transported to Troy finally came, and the Cochran brothers were ready. George and John gathered a couple of their friends, covered their faces with soot and staged an ambush outside of town in a thick wooded area. As the prisoner and his two escorts rode their horses by, a single shot rang out striking the prisoner and causing him to fall backwards. The horse spooked and started to run dragging the injured James Teagus behind him by his bonds. Mr. Teagus' head repeated smacked the ground as the deputy and constable who were escorting him tried to bring the spooked horse under control Finally the rope holding him to the horse broke and James Teagus fell to the ground.

The brothers and their friends rode past shooting at the wounded man, but they didn't slow down and every one of their shots missed. The prisoner's escorts picked up the man and made their way to a small cabin nearby, they tried to tend to his wounds, but he died three days later. Since the brothers and their friends had covered themselves with soot no one was able to identify them as the ones who had staged the ambush. And no one was ever prosecuted for the death of James M. Teagus.

Unfortunately the Cochran brothers were not done with their trouble making.

On July 16th, 1878 on the road between Auburn and New Hope, Missouri there was a grand picnic. It was one of those picnics were everyone would come out to socialize, the farmers and their families, the shop owners and theirs, the politicians, and all the townsfolk. A few days prior to the picnic Edward W. Rector had been in the Cochran's General Store causing all sorts of trouble. No one is quite sure the reason for Mr. Rector's outburst, but he had threatened George's life and thrown goods all over the store. George and John had been waiting for the right time to settle the score, and when they saw Mr. Rector at the picnic they knew that this was the time.

John immediately went to Mr. Rector and accused him of threatening his brother, George. Mr. Rector took John's accusation as a threat and a fight instantly broke out. The two men ended up on the ground, where Mr. Rector grabbed a large rock with the supposed intention of cracking John Cochran over the head with it. George saw what was happening, drew his gun, pointed for Mr. Rector's head and pulled the trigger. Mr. Rector fell to the ground dead as people began screaming and running away. The brothers fled the picnic and in the chaos were able to escape, and though the deputies pursued the Cochran brothers had too many friends that kept them well hid.

The next day John Cochran went to the sheriff's office and turned himself in. George Cochran was never heard from again, locals believed that he fled to family out of state. John later went to trial and was found innocent of the killing as there were many witnesses whom saw his brother kill the man. Edward W. Rector left behind a wife and four children. No one was ever found guilty of his murder.

1 Timothy 5:8
"But if anyone does not provide for his own, and especially for those of his household, he has denied the faith and is worse than an unbeliever."

Norman McFadden

25

The Legend of Auburn, Missouri 3

Samuel Gladney, his wife and their four children fought their way through 'hell and high water' to get to the government grant land that they were going to settle on. They left St. Charles, Missouri on March 4, 1820 and fought the bitter March winds all the way to Troy, where they stayed for a few nights to overcome their exhaustion and hunger.

Samuel's wife and oldest son took turns driving the wagon that held everything the family owned while Samuel and the other children hacked and chopped their way through the tangled Missouri backwoods to make a path wide enough for the wagon to pass through. On April 2, 1820 they pulled the wagon onto a big hill about twelve miles north of Troy, Missouri. Samuel and his oldest boy headed down the other side of that hill to scout out what was ahead of them.

It was slow going, but they finally made it to the hollow at the bottom. To their surprise there was a clean running spring in the hollow. It was late and everyone was tired but they headed back up then began clearing a path for the wagon to follow down. The sun was quickly overtaken by the darkness but Samuel and his son worked hard by lamplight to get the wagon to the bottom On the way down the youngest boy slipped and broke his ankle. They did what they could to set the bone and continued making their way to the hollow. Finally, they made it to the bottom by the spring, gathered up some firewood and settled in for the night.

One of the family would keep watch while the others slept because they knew there were mountain lions, wolves and even savage Indians in the area. But the night was without event. By the morning light Samuel checked the map of where their property was. A big smile spread across his face as he told his family the good news. According to the map they were right in the edge of their property.

The family decided that since the spring was right there, that it would be best to go ahead and build their cabin in the same spot. Immediately they set to the hard work of clearing the land and building a cabin. The winter was hard that first year and they lost their youngest child a three-year-old girl. But the prospered through the struggle.

The property that they settle was just down the hill from what became Auburn, Missouri. Samuel Gladney was born July 9th, 1789 in South Carolina, he died August 9th 1875 in Lincoln County, Missouri at the age of 86. He lived in his homestead for 55 years before his death. This man made it possible, through his hardships, and loss of family members, for us to call Lincoln County home. Samuel Gladney, the people of Lincoln County, Missouri salute you.

Proverbs 46:1-3

"God is our refuge and strength, A very present help in trouble. Therefore we will not fear, Even though the earth be removed, and though the mountains be carried into the midst of the sea; Though its waters roar and be troubled, though the mountains shake with its swelling."

26

The Gem Theater

You can't tell a story about the heart unless you tell a story about the body. The body that I am referring to is the little town of Elsberry, Missouri. But I have to tell you the history of Elsberry, before you can understand the heart of the town.

The year was 1673 when some boats came down the Big Muddy River looking for where it emptied into the Pacific Ocean. Father Marquette and Louis Joliet with five french voyagers stepped where no white man had ever stepped before, in what later became Elsberry, Missouri. Of course the Native Americans had been there.

Many years later on June 26th, 1812 the Sauk and the Fox Indians gathered in St. Charles, Missouri to sign a treaty with the United States government. In 1816 Lincoln County, Missouri became part of that treaty.. Then it was in the year 1863 when Robert T. Elsberry purchased 103 acres in Lincoln County right along the Mississippi River.

In 1879 three businessmen from Clarksville, Missouri started the Clarksville and Western Railroad Company. Their rail line ran between Clarksville, Missouri and Dardenne, Missouri (which is now St. Peters, Missouri). A group of land owners along the river decided that the railroad needed to build a depot on their land. In 1879 a depot was built on Robert Elsberry's land. It seemed almost overnight when the depot was built and three small villages came together; Lost Creek; Cross

Road; and Nelson, and the town of Elsberry, Missouri was platted.

But that's enough about the body, let's get on to the lifeline, the heart of Elsberry. Back in 1911 history was being created, and a legend was being born. No one knew at the time, but the heartbeat of Elsberry, Missouri had just been opened. The Gem Theater.

It was the longest lasting one screen cinema in Missouri, having been operating almost constantly from 1911 though 2022. Many things have happened in those years, they haven't been without trial and challenge. In 1930 a fire raged through the building all but destroying it. The owners quickly rebuilt, but another fire destroyed their efforts in 1937. It was as if something was trying to make the theater fail. But the owners fought through and rebuilt it again.

In 1950 the theater was sold and renamed The Senate Theater, and sold again in 1975 to its current owners Bob and Sandra Sinnett. Sadly tragedy struck again and another fired ravaged the theater on January 5th, 2011. Sadly the owners had no money to rebuild. But the little town of Elsberry came to the rescue! Everyone in the community chipped in and donated to the cause of rebuilding the theater. It seems as if nothing can keep this little theater from going on. The heart still beats in Elsberry, Missouri, if you have a free afternoon go visit the one screen theater, take in a movie and be taken back in time.

Ecclesiastes 3:1-8

"To every thing there is a season, and a time to every purpose under heaven: A time to be born, and a time to die; a time to plant, and a time to reap; A time to kill, and a time to heal; A time to break down, and a time to build up; A time to weep, and a time to laugh; A time to mourn and a time to dance; A time to cast away stones, and a time to gather stones together; A time to embrace, and a time to refrain from embracing; A time to get, and a time to lose; A time to keep, and a time to cast away; A time to rend, and a time to sew; A time to keep silence, and a time to speak; A time to love, and a time to hate; A time of war, and a time of peace."

Norman McFadden

ABOUT THE AUTHOR

Norman McFadden is the Author of the "Legends of Leeper holler" series. A licensed Minister and former pro wrestler, Norman resides in Lincoln County, Missouri, where he continues to write and do various works in ministry. For more information about the Author, visit Polstonhouse.com today!

Norman McFadden

AVAILABLE FROM POLSTONHOUSE.COM

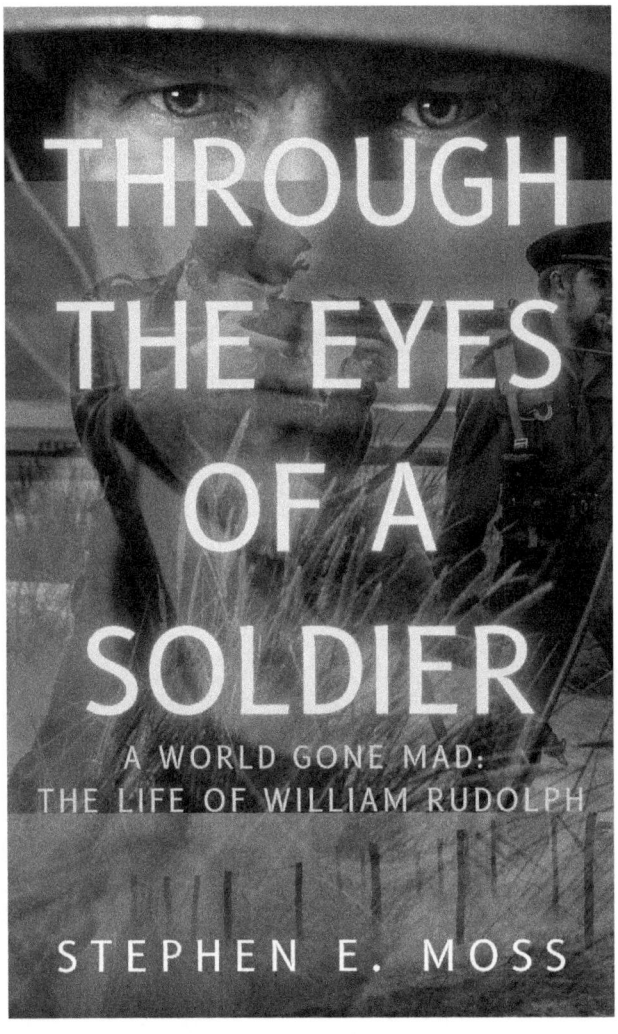

Norman McFadden

AVAILABLE FROM POLSTONHOUSE.COM

Norman McFadden

Norman McFadden

AVAILABLE FROM POLSTONHOUSE.COM

Norman McFadden

AVAILABLE FROM POLSTONHOUSE.COM

Norman McFadden

AVAILABLE FROM POLSTONHOUSE.COM

Norman McFadden

AVAILABLE FROM POLSTONHOUSE.COM

Norman McFadden

AVAILABLE FROM POLSTONHOUSE.COM

Norman McFadden

Urban Legends of Lincoln County, Missouri Volume 2.0

AVAILABLE FROM POLSTONHOUSE.COM

Norman McFadden

AVAILABLE FROM POLSTONHOUSE.COM

Norman McFadden